For Jo and Stevie

First published in Great Britain in 1993
by Simon & Schuster Young Books
This edition published in 2001 by Hodder Children's Books

10 9 8 7 6 5 4 3 2

A Catalogue record for this book is available from the British Library

ISBN 0 340 79519 0

Printed by Wing King Tong, Hong Kong

Hodder Children's Books
A Division of Hodder Headline Limited
338 Euston Road, London NW1 3BH

MICHAEL MORPURGO

THE KING IN THE FOREST

Illustrated by TONY KERINS

Hodder
Children's
Books

a division of Hodder Headline Limited

Chapter One

Deep in the forest there lived a charcoal-burner
and his son Tod. They were poor people but if
they worked hard there was just enough food to
feed themselves, their cow and their donkey.

Once a month Tod's father would load up the
donkey with charcoal and take it into town to
sell it in the market, and so Tod would be left on
his own to milk the cow, chop the wood and
keep the charcoal ovens burning.

One fine morning with his father gone into
town, Tod was out chopping wood when he
heard the sound of hunting horns echoing
through the forest. The King would be out
hunting again as he often was.

As the baying of the hounds came ever closer Tod looked up from his chopping. Something was moving at the edge of the forest, something white and small.

He put down his axe and ran over to see what it was, and there trembling in the high bracken was a fawn, a white fawn. The hounds and the horns were sounding all about him now, and he could see the huntsmen riding through the trees.

Swiftly he gathered the fawn in his arms and ran back inside the cottage.

Once inside he jumped into bed, still cradling the fawn, and pulled the blankets up over his nose. He lay there and held his breath. Outside he could hear the horses snorting and pawing the ground.

Then the hounds were whining and scratching at the door. Beside him he could feel the fawn panting under his hand.

Suddenly the door was thrown open, and the
King was standing there all muddy from the
chase. He came into the room, the huntsmen
behind him.

"We were hunting the white fawn, boy," he
said. "The hounds led us here to your cottage
door." He was looking around the room.

"I am not well," said Tod, the blanket still over his nose. "I have been in bed all day and have seen nothing, Sire. I have spots all over me. The pox, I think."

"The pox!" cried the King, backing away and covering his mouth.

"The pox!" cried the huntsmen; and within seconds the cottage was quite empty.

"You'll be all right now," said Tod, lifting the blanket, and the fawn touched Tod's ear with his cold, wet nose. It tickled and Tod laughed.

Then someone else was laughing behind him. By the bed stood a young girl with glowing cheeks and long red hair. She reached out and stroked the fawn tenderly.

"Daughter!" It was the King calling from outside. "Where are you?"

"You will not tell?" Tod whispered from behind his blanket.

"I will not tell," said the Princess and she smiled at him and was gone.

When Tod's father came back that night he found the white fawn curled up asleep at the bottom of the oven. "It's the warmest place," said Tod. And he told him the whole story.

"I can keep him, can't I, Father?" he said.

"He's a wild thing," said his father. "You cannot keep a wild thing, not for long. But neither can you throw him to the huntsmen. You may keep him."

Chapter Two

So the white fawn stayed and grew up with Tod.
Like brothers they walked and played together
in the woods and streams, never straying too far
from the cottage just in case the huntsmen came
back.

But whenever the hunting horn sounded, the
donkey would bray and the cow would bellow
and the fawn would come running for the safety
of the cottage and hide.

And Tod would watch at the window as they rode by, hoping to see again the sweet, glowing face of the Princess. But she never came.

She came in his dreams, though. She would be riding a white stag through the forest and she would be smiling at him.

So the long
years passed and Tod
grew to be a man, and
the white fawn became
a great white stag. Now he
would wander off alone for days
into the forest. If the hunting horns sounded the
donkey would bray for him and the cow would
bellow. But he only came back when he pleased,
and then the time came when he never came
back at all.

Tod was sad, of course, but he knew it was how it had to be, that his father was right, that wild things will be wild.

He was sadder still when his father grew old and died and he was left on his own.

Every month he went off to the town to sell his charcoal just as his father had, and he always passed by the castle gates hoping for a glimpse of the Princess, but he never saw her.

Chapter Three

Then one morning, he was at the market when the King rode by with his huntsmen, a terrible look on his face.

"Why does the King look so angry?" asked Tod.

"Have you not heard?" they said. "It is because of the King in the Forest?"

"The King in the Forest?"

"A great white stag," they told him, "one who wears a crown of horns wider than a man's reach. Ten years the King has been after him but, try as he might, he cannot catch him."

As Tod passed the castle gates that evening on his way home he heard the trumpets sounding on the ramparts. The whole town came running and the King came out to speak to them.

"No kingdom can have two kings," he thundered. "I would be rid of this so called 'King in the Forest'. Therefore I proclaim that whosoever brings me the antlers of the great white stag shall marry my daughter, and so rule my kingdom after me."

All night long Tod searched the forest calling for the white stag to warn him, to save him. All night long the donkey brayed and the cow bellowed, but he did not come and he did not come.

Dawn came and Tod heard the hunting horns
sounding through the forest. He went home.
There was nothing more he could do.

All that day he sat on the steps of his cottage,
his hands over his ears so that he need not hear
the terrible baying of the hounds.

It was almost sundown before Tod looked up
and as he did so saw the white stag stumbling
out of the bracken, the hounds close behind him.
He splashed wearily through the pond and
struggled up towards the cottage.

He tried to go in at the door but his antlers were too wide. He turned to face the hounds, and there was Tod, swinging his axe around his head, keeping the hounds at bay.

"The roof," cried Tod. "Get on the roof. They cannot reach you there."

The white stag summoned up his last strength and ran and leapt. With one bound he was on the roof.

Then, from out of the trees all around came the huntsmen, each one drawing an arrow from his quiver and taking careful aim.

"No!" cried Tod. "My house is mine, what is in my house is mine, what is on my house is mine. Call off your hounds and go home." And he spoke so strongly that no man amongst them dared argue.

When they were gone the white stag jumped down and came to him and put his cold wet nose against his ear and rested his great head on his shoulder.

"Dear friend," said Tod, "I have only to take your crown of horns and I could then marry the Princess of my dreams, but I cannot kill what I love. I cannot."

The white stag looked long at Tod. He took a
deep breath and began to shake his head
furiously. He lowered his antlers to the ground
and twisted and turned this way and that, his
horns stuck firmly in the earth.

And then at last he knelt down in front of
Tod. Tod took the antlers one in each hand and
felt they were loose. A gentle shake of the head
and they were free.

"Thank you, dear friend," said Tod, but the
white stag was already gone, a white shadow in
the gathering dark.

Chapter Four

Tod rose early the next morning, strapped the antlers to the donkey and set off for the town. As he rode through the streets word soon got about that the King in the Forest was dead, that Tod was on his way to the castle to claim the Princess as his bride.

A huge crowd followed him up to the castle
gates. The King heard them coming and came
out to meet them, the Princess beside him.

Tod bowed low.

"Look and see and know," said the King, holding high the antlers for the world to see, "that I am once more King again in my own land, and the only King too. By your clothes you are a poor man but a King's word is his bond, you shall have the reward I promised."

He took his daughter's hand and gave it to Tod. "You shall be married this very day, and when I am dead you shall be King in my place."

But when Tod, his heart full of happiness, looked down into the Princess's eyes, those eyes he had loved for so long, there was no smile for him, only a cold stoney stare.

She said nothing to him all through the marriage and indeed would scarcely look at him.

"It is because I am poor that you hate me so," he said when they were alone at last.

"Not so," she cried, the tears running down her cheeks. "It is because I have been forced to marry a man I do not love. I have loved, and will only ever love, one man. He was a charcoal-burner's son and I saw him just once a long time ago when I was a girl. I saw only his eyes, but they were eyes I shall never forget, not as long as I live. Never, do you hear me?"

And she went on, her eyes blazing: "And do you know what he was doing? He was hiding a white fawn under his blankets. The charcoal-burner's son and me, we saved it from the hunt. And that white fawn was the white stag you have just killed."

Tod hid his joy inside him as best he could. He thought to tell her there and then who he was, he longed to, but he knew she would not believe him. Why should she?

"Come," he said. "We shall live in my house. Castles are not for me. We shall return when duty calls us."

The donkey was waiting for them below in the courtyard, and so were the King and the Queen. They tried all they could to persuade him to stay and live in the castle.

"I promise one thing, Sire," said Tod. "If once she has seen it, your daughter does not wish to stay in my house, then I shall bring her back to you at once. You have my word, and like a King, a poor man's word is his bond."

So the King agreed and they let down the drawbridge and watched them leave, the Princess riding on the donkey.

Chapter Five

All the way home the donkey brayed loudly.
The Princess, pale and silent, hung her head in
misery. In the evening they came at last into the
clearing by the cottage, the pond gold with the
dying sun.

"This is my home," he said.

The Princess lifted her head and looked about her. "But I have been here before," she said. "I know I have."

"Perhaps you have," said Tod; and he helped her down off the donkey and led her towards the cottage door.

Still braying, the donkey ran down towards
the pond and the cow bellowed from the barn.

"Why is the donkey braying?" asked the
Princess. "And why is the cow bellowing?"

"I think they are calling a friend," said Tod.
"A friend who lives in the forest. If we stay and
watch a while, he will come. I know he will."

And sure enough, a few moments later, the great white stag came out of the trees and walked towards them across the clearing, the donkey beside him.

"The white stag," whispered the Princess. "The King in the Forest. But I thought you had killed him!"

"He gave me his antlers, his crown of horns," said Tod. "I could not kill him. He is my best friend, my oldest friend. After all, I have known him as long as I have known you, to the very day."

44

And the Princess, her face radiant with joy, smiled into his eyes, the smile he remembered so well. "And you have the eyes of the charcoal-burner's son," she said, "and I have found again the Prince of my heart."

And the white stag and the donkey walked
down to the golden pond and drank together
while Tod taught the Princess how to milk her
first cow. And they were as happy together as it
is possible to be.

Other titles by Michael Morpurgo from Hodder Children's Books . . .

Red Eyes at Night
Illustrated by Tony Ross

Millie's cousin Geraldine is a show-off and a pain.
Anything Millie can do, Geraldine can do better. Only one thing
will keep her quiet. And that's a ghost with bright red eyes.
A ghost lurking in the garden shed.
A ghost with a surprise in store for them all . . .

For older readers:

Robin of Sherwood

In this magical, spine-tingling story, the heroic tale
of Robin Hood is told as never before. After a fierce storm,
a boy of today discovers a human skull beneath the roots of
an upturned oak tree – and is suddenly thrown into the ancient
world of Sherwood Forest. Facing poverty, Robin joins the Outcasts,
a motley bunch of misfits who are both feared and hated for their
differences. But it is with these creatures of the forest that Robin
finds his own strength and courage, and his love, Maid Marian,
who gives him the power to fight his oppressors.

Look out for another acclaimed retelling of a classic story
by Michael Morpurgo – ***Joan of Arc**.*

HODDER

These colour story books are short, accessible novels for newly confident readers

JOAN AIKEN
Winner of the Guardian Fiction Award

The
SHOEMAKER'S
BOY

Illustrated by ALAN MARKS

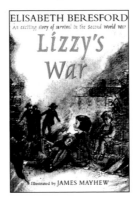

ELISABETH BERESFORD
An exciting story of survival in the Second World War

Lizzy's
War

Illustrated by JAMES MAYHEW

ELISABETH BERESFORD
The exciting sequel to LIZZY'S WAR

Lizzy
Fights On

Illustrated by JAMES MAYHEW

LEON GARFIELD
Winner of the Whitbread Children's Book Award

Fair's
Fair

Illustrated by BRIAN HOSKIN

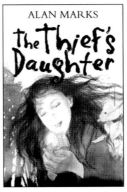

ALAN MARKS

the Thief's
Daughter

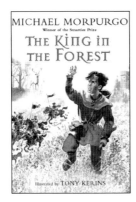

MICHAEL MORPURGO
Winner of the Smarties Prize

THE KING IN
THE FOREST

Illustrated by TONY KERINS

JILL PATON WALSH
By the Smarties prize-winning author of *Thomas and the Tinners*

Birdy and the
Ghosties

Illustrated by ALAN MARKS

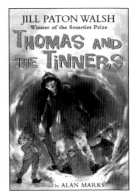

JILL PATON WALSH
Winner of the Smarties Prize

THOMAS AND
THE TINNERS

Illustrated by ALAN MARKS